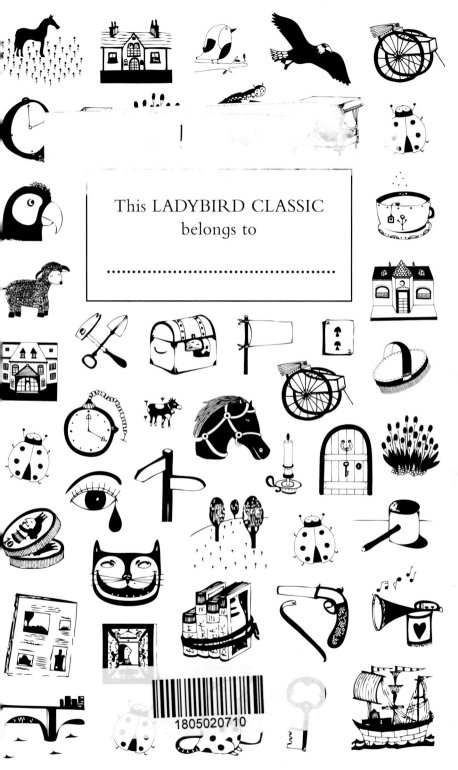

This LADYBIRD CLASSIC
belongs to

....

A History of the Author

Bram Stoker was born in Dublin in
1847. In the 1870s, the famous English
actor Sir Henry Irving offered Stoker
a job at his production company at the
Lyceum Theatre in London's West End.
This inspired his creative writing.

In 1897, Stoker published his masterpiece,
Dracula. It was successful at the time and
continues to grow in popularity today.

Chapter illustrations by Valeria Valenza

LADYBIRD BOOKS

UK | USA | Canada | Ireland | Australia

India | New Zealand | South Africa

Ladybird Books is part of the Penguin Random House group of companies
whose addresses can be found at global.penguinrandomhouse.com.

First published 2015

001

Copyright © Ladybird Books Ltd, 2015

Ladybird and the Ladybird logo are registered trademarks owned by Ladybird Books Ltd

The moral right of the author and illustrators has been asserted

Printed in China

A CIP catalogue record for this book is available from the British Library

ISBN: 978–0–723–29705–5

LADYBIRD CLASSICS

Dracula

By Bram Stoker

Retold by Joan Cameron
Illustrated by Matthew Land

Contents

CHAPTER ONE

Journey to Castle Dracula

MIDNIGHT WAS APPROACHING
as the carriage wound its way through
a wooded pass, deep in the Carpathian
Mountains. Jonathan Harker, a young
English solicitor, lay dozing in his seat,
exhausted. The journey from England had
been a long one and, since his arrival in
Transylvania, an eerie one, too.

A wolf howled in the distance and

Jonathan stirred uneasily. He had heard much talk of wolves, vampires and witches in this lovely but strange country. Only the night before, the innkeeper's wife had been horrified to hear where he was going. 'Castle Dracula!' she had gasped. 'Must you go?'

'Yes, I must,' Jonathan had replied. 'Count Dracula has bought an estate in London, and I have papers for him to sign. He is sending a carriage to collect me tomorrow.'

The old woman had hesitated, then fastened her own crucifix round his neck. 'Then wear this, for your mother's sake!'

Puzzled, but wanting to please her, Jonathan had agreed. He could feel the cross now, under his shirt.

Suddenly the carriage stopped. Jonathan's heart leapt in fright. Wolves were all around, teeth gleaming, tongues lolling. All at once, they began to howl.

The black-cloaked driver jumped down. He gave one wave of his arms and the wolves melted away into the darkness. He took Jonathan's bag from the rack and opened the carriage door. 'Castle Dracula,' he said.

Jonathan got out. Before him lay a vast, ruined castle, its broken battlements a jagged line against the sky. Not a light showed. Behind him, the carriage rattled away. He was alone.

CHAPTER TWO

Jonathan Meets the Count

JONATHAN WAITED. BEFORE him stood a great door, studded with iron nails. Should he knock? It seemed an age before the door grated open.

A tall man stood in the doorway, dressed in black from head to foot.

'I am Count Dracula,' he said. His English was good, but he had a strange accent. 'Welcome to my house, Mr Harker.

Enter freely and of your own will.'

Following the Count into a well-lit room, Jonathan found his fears vanishing. A log fire blazed in the hearth, and a table was set for supper. The Count opened another door, revealing a comfortable bedroom. 'This is your room, Mr Harker. First, please eat. Excuse me if I do not join you. I have already dined.'

While Jonathan ate, the Count asked many questions about the journey. Afterwards they sat by the fire. The Count's questions continued. This time he asked about Carfax, the estate he had purchased in London, and he signed the documents Jonathan had brought. Hours passed, and still he talked. Dawn was breaking when Count Dracula finally stood up.

'Sleep as long as you wish, Mr Harker,' he said. 'You may go anywhere in the castle, except where doors are locked.

I must warn you, however – sleep only in your own room. Transylvanian ways are not English ways.'

Jonathan was so tired that he thought nothing of this strange warning. He slept late into the next day. When he awoke, he found a cold meal waiting. There was no sign of Count Dracula and there were no servants in sight. He looked around for a bell to summon the servants but couldn't find one.

Dracula did not appear until evening. When he did, the young solicitor asked about his journey home, as his business was completed.

'You must not go yet, my friend!' cried the Count. 'You came to settle details of my new estate, Carfax. Now I must learn about London. How I long to walk through her crowded streets! I know of her only through books. Tell me more!'

Once again, the Count questioned

Jonathan far into the night. Only with the coming dawn did he allow Jonathan to fall into bed, exhausted.

The same pattern repeated itself for days. In daylight, the Count was nowhere to be seen, and Jonathan slept. By night, the Count was with him, talking endlessly. Jonathan never saw him eat or drink.

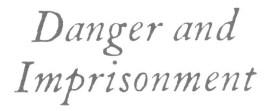

CHAPTER THREE

Danger and Imprisonment

ONE EVENING, JONATHAN was
shaving when Dracula came unexpectedly
into the room. He was not reflected in
Jonathan's mirror!

Startled, Jonathan let his hand slip and
cut himself. The Count's eyes blazed at the
sight of the blood, and he started forward.

Suddenly he drew back. He had seen
the crucifix at Jonathan's throat.

'Take care how you cut yourself,' he snarled. 'It can be more dangerous than you think in this country.'

Then, just like that, the Count was gone. Trembling, Jonathan went to the window seeking fresh air. The castle stood on the edge of a precipice. Looking down, Jonathan was just in time to see a figure emerging from a lower window. It was the Count. He was crawling down the castle wall, like a great bat.

Jonathan was filled with fear and dread. He needed to return to England and Mina, the girl he was going to marry.

Escape was not so easy, though. The great main door was locked and, although Jonathan searched, he could find no other way out. He was a prisoner!

As he went on searching, he eventually found himself in a room he had not visited before.

He was worn out, and lay down on a

silken couch, ignoring the Count's warning not to to sleep anywhere but in his own room.

CHAPTER FOUR

The Attack

TIME PASSED. SUDDENLY, Jonathan was not alone. The room was the same, with only his footprints clearly marked on the dusty floor. Yet three beautiful women had appeared through a misty shaft of moonlight. They cast no shadows. All three had brilliant white teeth and ruby-red lips.

Jonathan was filled with deadly fear, but he could not move.

One of the women bent over him and he felt her sharp teeth fasten on his throat. In that instant, another presence was in the room. It was Count Dracula.

With a fierce sweep of his arm, he threw the woman away from Jonathan, and waved the others back with the same gesture the carriage driver had used against the wolves.

'How dare you touch him?' Dracula hissed. 'This man is mine! When I am done with him, then you may have him!'

'Are we to have nothing tonight?' one of the women wailed.

Dracula pointed to a bag on the floor. It moved as if something alive was inside, and Jonathan thought he heard the muffled cry of a child.

The women bent over the bag eagerly, mouths open, teeth glistening. They were about to feed on the blood of a child!

It was too much. Jonathan fainted.

CHAPTER FIVE

An Attempt to Escape

DAYLIGHT WAS CREEPING through the castle windows when Jonathan regained consciousness. He was alone once more, but was still filled with fear. He had to escape, and there was a way, if he dared take it! Dracula himself had climbed down the front of the castle wall. Jonathan made up his mind to do the same.

He stepped through the window on to

the ledge outside. Below lay a sheer drop over the precipice, but there were footholds in the rough stones of the castle wall.

While he had the courage, Jonathan began the climb, trying not to look down.

Some time later, he came to the Count's room, too tired to go any further. The room was empty, and he scrambled in through the window.

In one corner, a door led to a dark staircase. Jonathan cautiously followed it downwards, and found himself in a dimly lit crypt. The floor had been freshly dug over and great boxes, filled with earth, lay around. He counted fifty in all. In one of them, Jonathan saw something which filled him with horror. The Count was lying there!

He was not breathing, and had no heartbeat, yet his face was gorged with blood. His lips were stained with it, and

drops ran down his chin. Like the three terrible women, this creature fed on human blood. And he was going to London, with all its millions of innocent people. He had to be stopped!

Snatching up a shovel, Jonathan struck out at the evil face. As he did so, the head turned towards him, dead eyes blazing with hate. The shovel twisted in Jonathan's hands so that the blow to the Count was only a glancing one.

Dropping the shovel in terror, Jonathan rushed from the crypt, away from the monster that was Dracula.

Jonathan found himself back in the Count's room. The door to the staircase slammed behind him and, when he tried it, it wouldn't open. A feeling of despair came over him. Just then, he heard the rolling of heavy wheels in the castle courtyard, and the sound of merry voices. There was hope!

A tiny window overlooked the courtyard,

and he peered out. A band of gypsies had arrived. They seemed to know of some secret way into the castle, for they were bringing out the boxes from the crypt, and loading them on to their wagons.

Try as he might, Jonathan could not attract their attention. They finished loading. The heavy wheels began to turn and, singing all the way, the gypsies left.

'Come back!' Jonathan cried in despair. 'Help me!'

They were gone. His heart sank. He knew that Dracula lay hidden in one of those boxes. Was this the first stage of the Count's journey to Carfax, his new estate in London?

Now Jonathan was alone in the castle with those three terrifying women, and soon they would be looking for more blood. 'Oh, Mina,' he groaned. 'Will I ever see you again?'

He got to his feet, determined. He would try to climb down the castle wall to the valley below. Then he would leave this cursed land and return to England.

CHAPTER SIX

Strange Happenings in England

FAR AWAY IN England, Mina Murray, Jonathan's fiancée, had just arrived in the Yorkshire town of Whitby. Her friend Lucy Westenra had a holiday house there where they were enjoying a break.

Lucy could hardly wait to tell Mina her news. She had received three marriage proposals in one day! All three of the men were close friends.

The first, Dr John Seward, was a clever young physician who was in charge of a London psychiatric hospital. The second man was an American from Texas, Quincey P. Morris. The third suitor was the Honourable Arthur Holmwood – and she had accepted him.

'We are to be married in the autumn!' she told Mina, blushing with happiness.

Time passed pleasantly in Whitby. The two friends spent their time walking along the cliffs or sitting in the sun, looking out over the town's rooftops to the sea. Sometimes they talked to the coastguard, or to an old fisherman.

July passed into August, and Mina began to worry. She had received only a brief note from Jonathan, and Transylvania was so far away. To make matters worse, Lucy had begun to have nightmares, and also she would sleepwalk! Mina could not understand why.

One fine afternoon, as they sat talking to the old fisherman, a dark cloud covered the sun.

A cold wind blew in from the sea, and the old fisherman suddenly cried, 'There's something in that wind! It smells like death!'

By late evening, the clouds had drawn together in the sky. The sunset was so beautiful that people gathered on the clifftops to watch. Mina and Lucy were among them. Without warning, a storm broke. The sea raged, and the wind roared.

'Look at that ship!' cried the old fisherman, pointing.

A schooner, all sails set, was driving through the huge waves, heading for the shore. As it drew closer, the watching crowds gasped. A dead man was secured to the helm.

The schooner rushed on, and drove hard on to the beach with a mighty crash.

At that instant, a huge dog sprang up from below decks and leapt on to the sand. The crowds watched it race up the hillside towards the old churchyard. There it disappeared amongst the tombstones.

All of a sudden, the sky was dark. Lucy shuddered.

'It's time we went home,' Mina said, taking her arm.

CHAPTER SEVEN

Lucy's Mysterious Illness

THE EXCITEMENT OF the night was not over. Lucy seemed disturbed, and fell into a restless sleep. Around midnight, she left the house, walking in her sleep. Mina heard her go, and, throwing on her dressing gown, ran after her.

As Mina reached the old churchyard, she saw Lucy sitting on a seat near the gate. Then she caught sight of a dark figure bending over her friend.

'Lucy! Lucy!' she called out in fright.
The figure looked up, and Mina saw a
white face and staring eyes. Then it was
gone. Lucy was in a daze, and there were
strange marks at her throat, but somehow
Mina got her friend back to the house
and into bed.

The next day started well, with clear
skies, and Lucy seemed herself again. In
the morning, they strolled down to the
beach, where the stricken schooner still
lay. Men were unloading great boxes from
her hold. The coastguard looked on.

'Good morning, ladies,' he greeted
them.

'Was anyone saved from the ship?'
Mina asked.

'There was no one aboard but the
captain,' he replied, shaking his head.
'He was dead. The vessel came from the
Balkan port of Varna, loaded with these

boxes. They are addressed to a house in London, so we're sending them on.' He shook his head again. 'It's a strange affair.'

Mina soon forgot about the wrecked schooner. A letter arrived later that morning from Budapest. Jonathan was safe, but in hospital there. He was in poor health, following some frightening experience in Transylvania.

'Mr Harker has had some fearful shock,' the letter explained. 'He is recovering well, and asking for you.'

'I must go to him!' Mina cried. 'Will you be all right, Lucy?'

'Of course you must go,' Lucy said. 'It's time I returned to London in any case. Arthur will be expecting me.'

Some time after Lucy's return to London, Arthur Holmwood called on his friend, Dr Seward. A specialist in mental illnesses, John Seward had a house attached to a psychiatric hospital.

The friends often met there.

'I'm puzzled about Renfield, one of my patients,' John Seward told the other man, as they sat talking. 'I thought he was cured, but now he is acting so oddly.'

'In what way?'

'Last night he broke out of here, and was found trying to get into Carfax – the house next door. It's a big place, with an old chapel attached, but it's empty. When we got him back to his room, he kept telling us, "The Master is at hand". Then he lay in bed, smiling, watching a big bat flap around outside his window. Very odd behaviour. A pity, as it had seemed he was getting better.'

John looked quizzically at his friend. 'But something is troubling you, Arthur. What is it?'

'It's Lucy,' Arthur said. 'She's not at all well, and I can't find out what's wrong. Will you see her?'

'Of course.'

Dr Seward saw the girl the next day. Apart from looking a little pale, he could find nothing wrong with her. Yet she was certainly far from well. He sent a note to Arthur Holmwood.

'I'm concerned about Lucy,' it said. 'I have asked Professor Van Helsing to come from Amsterdam to see her. He is an old friend of mine, and an expert on mystery illnesses. Perhaps he can help Lucy with her own.'

CHAPTER EIGHT

Van Helsing
Comes to Help

BY THE TIME Professor Van Helsing
arrived from Amsterdam, Lucy had
become very weak. Her face was
chalk-white, her lips bloodless. The
Dutchman examined her, and his face
changed when he found marks on her
throat, under the velvet band she wore
round her neck. He took John Seward
to one side.

'She must have a blood transfusion at once,' he said.

'What's wrong with her?' Seward asked.

'I think I know, but I hope I am wrong,' the Dutchman replied. 'I must look through my books, and think. First, the transfusion. After that, keep garlic flowers in her room.'

'Garlic flowers?' The young doctor looked amazed. 'But why?'

'Trust me!' Van Helsing said. 'Do as I say, please.'

Mystified, John Seward agreed.

Lucy seemed better after the blood transfusion, but as the days passed she needed even more. Hearing of her illness, Quincey Morris came to offer his help. He was shocked to see the change in Lucy. She talked of bad dreams and of a great bat at her window. The friends could only watch as she slipped away from them.

Eventually, Lucy closed her eyes and

her breathing stopped. Arthur Holmwood was heartbroken.

'She is at peace at last,' John Seward said quietly. 'It is the end.'

'No, my friend.' Van Helsing turned to him. 'I fear this may only be the beginning.'

Lucy's funeral was over before Jonathan and Mina returned from Budapest. They had married there as soon as Jonathan had been well enough. The couple were saddened to hear of their friend's death.

Mina kept a close eye on Jonathan. She had been shocked to hear of his ordeal at Castle Dracula, and he had been very ill. Now he was beginning to look better.

The couple were walking along a London street one evening, when Jonathan suddenly stopped dead.

'What's wrong?' asked Mina anxiously.

Jonathan was staring across the street at a tall man with black hair. 'It's the Count!' he exclaimed. 'He's already here, in London.'

Jonathan was trembling. Worried, Mina hailed a hansom cab, and took him to Dr Seward's house. Fortunately, the doctor was at home, and Professor Van Helsing was with him. The two medical men listened in silence while Mina told them everything.

'Did I imagine it all?' Jonathan asked in a low voice.

'No, my friend, you did not,' said Van Helsing firmly. 'And your experiences would seem to have a link with Lucy's death. You say this evil being is now in London? We must hunt him out!'

'I'm with you!' Jonathan exclaimed.

The next morning, a London paper carried a frightening story of children being taken away by a 'beautiful lady'. They were found afterwards, alive but with puncture marks on their throats.

Van Helsing showed the paper to Dr Seward. 'What do you make of this?' he asked.

'Something attacked these children,' John Seward exclaimed. 'That something must also have attacked Lucy!'

'No, my friend.' Van Helsing shook his head. 'How can I make you understand how Lucy died? Listen, there are many strange things in this world. In some places there are giant bats which drink the blood of cattle and horses. Sometimes they even suck the blood of sailors sleeping on the decks of their ships. In the morning, the sailors are dead men, as white as Lucy was.'

John Seward stared at the Dutchman. 'Are you saying that such a thing is here in London? Lucy was bitten by a bat?'

'It is worse than that,' Van Helsing groaned. 'Lucy herself made the holes in the children's throats.'

'Are you mad? Lucy is dead!'

'I know that you do not believe me,' Van Helsing said sadly. 'But tonight, after dark, we must go to the churchyard where Lucy is buried. Then you will see. Then you will understand.'

CHAPTER NINE

The Un-dead

AFTER DARK, THE two men silently entered the crypt where Lucy's coffin lay. Carefully, Van Helsing opened it.

Dr Seward gave a startled gasp. The coffin was empty.

Van Helsing led him outside, gesturing to him to be silent. They waited behind a tree. As they watched, a figure flitted back into the crypt. It was Lucy.

Van Helsing took his companion by the arm and led him back into the crypt. Again, he opened the coffin. This time Lucy lay there, even more beautiful than she had been in life.

Van Helsing explained quietly. 'Lucy was bitten by a vampire while she was in a trance, sleepwalking. The vampire returned again and again for blood, and Lucy died. She is not really dead, but Un-dead. She has become like the vampire herself, and needs human blood. Her soul will not rest until a stake is driven through her heart.'

John Seward shuddered.

They returned the following night as midnight struck, this time with Arthur Holmwood and Quincey Morris. Silently, Van Helsing showed them the empty coffin while they waited for Lucy's return. She appeared quite suddenly, and somewhere behind her a child whimpered. By the light of a street lamp, they saw fresh blood on

Lucy's lips. Her face was evil.

'That is not my Lucy,' Arthur groaned. 'Van Helsing, we must help her to go to her rest.'

The deed was soon done. The stake was driven through the heart of the thing that was not Lucy. The creature screamed once. A look of peace then crossed its face. Lucy was Un-dead no more.

The friends gathered at John Seward's house to begin their search for Dracula. Before they began, Van Helsing told them what he knew of vampirism.

'A vampire can direct the weather and living things like bats and wolves,' he said. 'He is Un-dead. He can take any shape, casts no shadow or reflection, and can vanish at will. His powers are limited to the hours of darkness, and by day he must lie in a coffin or earth box. He can only enter a house if he is invited in by someone living there. Some things take his power away – garlic, a crucifix, sacred wafers from a church. Unless a stake is driven through his heart as he lies in his lair, he will live forever.'

There was a short silence. This was the terrible power they must defeat.

Van Helsing went on. 'It seems certain that Dracula, in the shape of a dog, came ashore from the wrecked schooner at Whitby. I've discovered that the boxes from the schooner were delivered to Carfax, the house next door to this, which the Count bought. Each box is a place of safety for him during daylight.'

'I had enough clues from the behaviour of Renfield,' said Seward grimly.

'Some of the boxes were taken away by carters yesterday,' Van Helsing continued. 'Renfield was much affected, screaming that they were stealing his "Master". We must now find the boxes that still remain next door at Carfax. If we sterilize them with sacred wafers, Dracula can never rest in them again. Then we must find the others, and do the same. First, Carfax!'

Mina got up to go with them, but Van Helsing put his hand on her arm. 'Stay here, Mina,' he said quietly. 'We need you to be safe.'

Led by Van Helsing, the men left Seward's house. Before they went into Carfax, the Dutchman gave each man a crucifix and a garland of garlic flowers.

'Keep these near your hearts,' he instructed them.

Quietly, by lamplight, they entered the dark house through a broken door. The whole place was thick with dust, and seemed deserted. Yet they all sensed an evil presence. They found the earth boxes in the old chapel adjoining the house. The air there was foul.

'There are twenty-nine boxes here,' said Quincey Morris.

Suddenly the floor at their feet was alive with rats. They came from nowhere, and multiplied until there were thousands of them. Arthur Holmwood gave a loud whistle. His three terriers ran in. As they rushed to attack, the rats vanished. With their departure, the evil presence seemed to go, too. Relieved, the men got on with the task of sterilizing the boxes.

From her bedroom in John Seward's house, Mina heard the dogs bark. All was dark outside. Mist began to whirl outside the window, and two red eyes seemed to peer in at her. Her last conscious memory was of a white face and two staring eyes.

Next morning, Mina was tired and pale, but her experience in the night seemed like a bad dream. She said nothing about it.

The friends continued their enquiries. The carters gave them the addresses in London where the boxes had been taken.

Soon all but nine boxes had been dealt with. Only one address was left – a house in Piccadilly.

Suddenly, Renfield screamed. The friends rushed to his room, and found him lying in a pool of blood. Just before he died, he whispered, 'I let him in. He has gone to take blood from Mina. When I saw what he was going to do, I tried to stop him, but his strength was too great…'

Now they knew where Dracula was! Rushing upstairs, the men burst in to Mina's room. Dracula was bent over her, and there was blood on her clothes.

The men advanced on the evil thing. Van Helsing, holding out a crucifix, drove him back, away from Mina. Abruptly he vanished, leaving Mina weeping.

'He will have to get to the house in Piccadilly before dawn to rest in one of his boxes,' exclaimed Van Helsing. 'We'll go there now, and wait for him.'

As soon as they entered the Piccadilly house, the friends knew Dracula had been there. The place smelt just like the old chapel at Carfax. In the dining room they found eight boxes, and quickly sterilized them with sacred wafers. There was just one box left, and they could find no trace of it.

'Where can it be?' cried Jonathan. Van Helsing shook his head. As they stood there, the front door opened, and slow, careful footsteps came along the hall. It was Count Dracula. He turned to look at them. His face twisted into a snarl, so that they could see his long pointed teeth.

'You think you have left me without a place to rest – but I have another. You shall all be sorry. I shall have my revenge!' With that, he was gone.

Disheartened, the friends returned to Seward's house. Mina was waiting for them, looking pale and anxious.

She became paler as they told her what had happened, and turned to Van Helsing.

'Professor, Dracula put me in a trance when he came to my room,' she said. 'If you also put me in a trance, perhaps my mind can sense where he is.'

Van Helsing looked at Jonathan, who nodded agreement. It was worth trying. Settling Mina in an armchair, the Dutchman began to hypnotize her. Gradually her eyes closed, and she began to speak. 'He is in a dark room. Water is lapping outside. It is a ship, and it is leaving port.'

Her voice faded away, and her breathing deepened.

'She's asleep,' said Van Helsing. 'That ship will be leaving from your great Port of London. But how many others will also be leaving?'

'Lloyd's will help us,' Arthur Holmwood told him. 'They will be able to tell us which ships are sailing, and where they are going.'

It was well into the day before they had the answer. From Lloyd's list, only one ship seemed to be heading in the right direction – the *Czarina Catherine*, which was bound for Varna, on the Black Sea. By the time they had reached the docks, however, she had sailed. A tall, mysterious man had been seen going aboard, and a huge wooden box had been loaded into the hold. Dracula had his earthbox, and he was escaping, back to Transylvania!

'We still have a chance,' Van Helsing pointed out. 'The journey by sea will take weeks. Travelling overland, we can be there in days.'

'Yes!' agreed Quincey Morris. 'We'll take the Orient Express and be there, waiting for him.'

Van Helsing took John Seward to one side.

'John, we must catch Dracula soon,' he said. 'Don't say anything to Jonathan, but Mina is changing. I can see the vampire signs beginning to show in her face.'

CHAPTER TEN

Daylight

THE JOURNEY TO Varna was
uneventful. Once there, they stayed at a
hotel and eagerly waited for news of the
Czarina Catherine.

'We will board the ship between sunrise
and sunset,' Van Helsing said. 'He cannot
leave in daylight. We will strike while he
lies in his lair.'

Soon afterwards, a message came from

the docks. Dracula had outwitted them! The *Czarina Catherine* had sailed on to Galatz, further to the north.

The friends took the first train to Galatz. When they got there, they heard that a huge box had been unloaded from the ship, and was on its way upriver in an open boat.

Van Helsing gave a cry of triumph. 'We will catch him yet. He cannot cross water by himself. As long as the box is on a running stream, he cannot leave it.'

Quickly, they made arrangements to follow. Arthur Holmwood and Jonathan Harker would follow the boat upriver in a hired steam launch. Dr Seward and Quincey Morris would go by horseback along the riverbank. Mina would be in Van Helsing's care. They would hire a carriage and drive to Castle Dracula through the Borgó Pass.

Mina became restless and troubled as

they neared Castle Dracula. 'He is near. I know he is near,' she murmured.

Night approached, and Van Helsing stopped the carriage. Using sacred wafers, he threw a holy ring around them. Then he lit a fire, for it was beginning to snow. Soon it was dark.

The horses began to scream. Wreaths of mist took the shape of three women in flowing dresses. Van Helsing felt fear touch his heart.

The women came closer. Van Helsing could see their red lips and pointed white teeth. They were the three women from Castle Dracula and they beckoned to Mina.

'Come, sister. Come with us,' they crooned.

Van Helsing and Mina were safe within the holy ring. The three women could not enter it.

They remained like that until dawn came. Van Helsing watched the three

women melt into the whirling mist and snow. The sun came up, and they were gone. Mina had fallen into a peaceful sleep.

Leaving her wrapped in blankets, safe within the holy ring, Van Helsing took the carriage. He drove like the wind to Castle Dracula. He broke into the castle and found his way to the ruined chapel. There the three women lay in three stone tombs, beautiful but Un-dead.

There was one more tomb, huge and more impressive than the rest. On it was but one word: DRACULA. Van Helsing laid some sacred wafers inside the tomb, banishing Dracula from it forever.

He then drove a stake through each of the women's hearts. Van Helsing saw peace cross each woman's face before her body turned to dust.

On the way out of the castle, he sealed all the entrances with sacred wafers.

The Count could no longer enter.

With one last look at Castle Dracula, Van Helsing drove back to Mina.

'Jonathan is coming!' she cried. 'But so is Dracula!'

The day passed slowly. Suddenly, they saw movement. A band of gypsies was racing towards them, and on one of their carts lay Dracula's huge box.

'They are racing for the sunset,' groaned Van Helsing.

'Look!' Mina exclaimed. 'Horsemen!'

Van Helsing stared for a moment, then shouted in glee. 'Quincey and John are coming, and Arthur and Jonathan are close behind!'

Now the gypsies were barely a hundred yards away. The four horsemen overtook them. Jonathan and Quincey threw themselves through the ring of gypsies, fighting off their flashing knives. With incredible strength, they raised the great

box and hurled it to the ground. It broke open. Seeing the men's rifles, the gypsies fell back.

Count Dracula lay in his earthbox, red eyes gleaming. The sun was almost down. In that instant, Quincey Morris plunged his knife deep into the Count's heart.

It was like a miracle. A fleeting look of peace passed over Dracula's face, then the body crumbled into dust and vanished. Castle Dracula stood out against the sky, every stone of its broken battlements etched against the light of the setting sun.

Quincey gave a groan, and sank to the ground. He had been stabbed by one of the gypsies' knives. His friends rushed to his side, and Mina took his hand.

'The curse has passed away,' he sighed. And, to his friends' bitter grief, he died.

His death was not in vain. The vampire signs were gone from Mina's face. She was safe. Count Dracula was gone forever.

Collect more fantastic
LADYBIRD CLASSICS

Alice in Wonderland

9781409311232

Oliver Twist

9781409311256

Treasure Island

9781409311287

BLACK BEAUTY

9781409311249

GULLIVER'S Travels

9781409311270

The Secret Garden

9781409311263

A Christmas Carol

9781409312215

Peter Pan

9781409312222

The Three Musketeers

9781409313557

THE WIND IN THE WILLOWS

9781409313564

Heidi

9781409313571

The Jungle Book

9781409313588

Little Women

9780723270874

The Railway Children

9780723270867

Robin Hood

9780723295594

KING ARTHUR

9780723295600

FRANKENSTEIN

9780723297062